Hello, Family Members,

Learning to read is one of the most importa[nt] of early childhood. **Hello Reader!** books a[re] children become skilled readers who like [to] readers learn to read by remembering frequently used words like "the," "is," and "and"; by using phonics skills to decode new words; and by interpreting picture and text clues. These books provide both the stories children enjoy and the structure they need to read fluently and independently. Here are suggestions for helping your child *before*, *during*, and *after* reading:

Before

- Look at the cover and pictures and have your child predict what the story is about.
- Read the story to your child.
- Encourage your child to chime in with familiar words and phrases.
- Echo read with your child by reading a line first and having your child read it after you do.

During

- Have your child think about a word he or she does not recognize right away. Provide hints such as "Let's see if we know the sounds" and "Have we read other words like this one?"
- Encourage your child to use phonics skills to sound out new words.
- Provide the word for your child when more assistance is needed so that he or she does not struggle and the experience of reading with you is a positive one.
- Encourage your child to have fun by reading with a lot of expression . . . like an actor!

After

- Have your child keep lists of interesting and favorite words.
- Encourage your child to read the books over and over again. Have him or her read to brothers, sisters, grandparents, and even teddy bears. Repeated readings develop confidence in young readers.
- Talk about the stories. Ask and answer questions. Share ideas about the funniest and most interesting characters and events in the stories.

I do hope that you and your child enjoy this book.

—Francie Alexander
Reading Specialist,
Scholastic's Learning Ventures

ISBN 0-439-18300-6

Library of Congress Cataloging-in-Publication Data available

10 9 8 7   01 02 03 04 05

Printed in the U.S.A.   24
First printing, January 2001

NORMAN BRIDWELL
Clifford's®
Valentines

Hello Reader! — Level 1

SCHOLASTIC INC.

New York   Toronto   London   Auckland   Sydney   Mexico City   New Delhi   Hong Kong

It is Valentine's Day.

Clifford gets a card.
It is from a boy.

Clifford gets a card.
It is from a girl.

Clifford gets a card
from a woman.

Clifford gets a card
from a man.

The letter carrier comes.

Now Clifford gets many, many more cards.
Everyone loves Clifford!

It starts to snow.

It snows and snows.
Clifford has an idea.

He runs to the park.

The boy, the girl, the woman,
and the man are there.

Many, many other people are there, too.

Clifford makes a heart in the snow.

WALLA WALLA
RURAL LIBRARY DISTRICT
TOUCHET

Happy Valentine's Day, everyone!

• Word List •

a	it
an	letter
and	loves
are	makes
boy	man
card	many
carrier	more
Clifford	now
comes	other
day	park
everyone	people
from	runs
gets	snow
girl	starts
happy	the
has	there
heart	to
idea	too
in	Valentine's
is	woman